Dedicated to the fine artists and naturalists of the 18th and 19th centuries whose devotion to pen and stylus created a golden age of black and white engravings that has never been equalled.

ISBN 0-932529-52-6

© A.B. Curtiss 1996   Library bound on acid-free paper   Printed in Hong Kong

First Edition 10 9 8 7 6 5 4 3 2

Curtiss, Arline B.
 Hallelujah, A Cat Comes Back/A.B. Curtiss
 p. cm.
 Summary: How cats with character must make their way through life's ups and downs and no matter how bad things are, a cat comes back!

ISBN 0-932529-52-6

1. Cats-Juvenile fiction. 2. Cats-fiction.
PZ8.3.C8785Ha 1996 {E}-dc20 Library of Congress Catalog Card Number: 95-74768

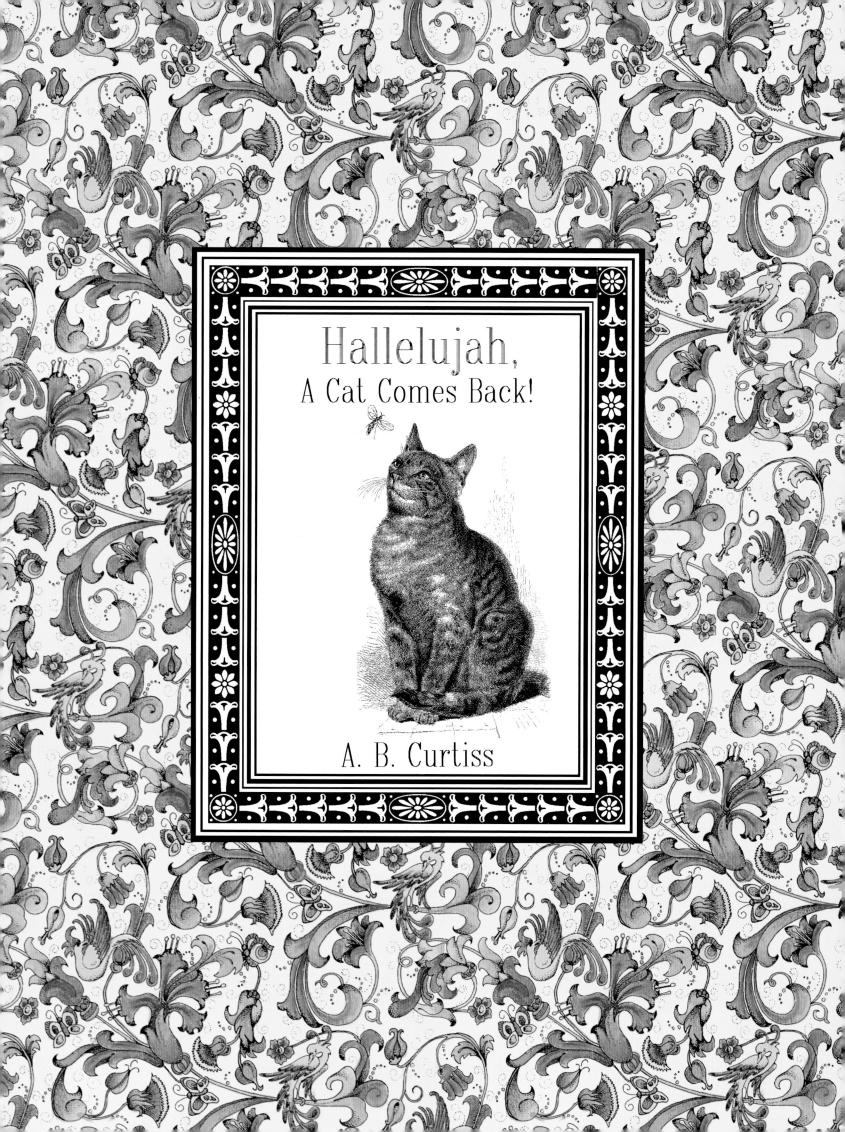

Hallelujah,
A Cat Comes Back!

A. B. Curtiss

The air was chill

and rustling with

the dry leaves of the Fall.

I turned around for one last look

And waved good-bye to all.

I was bolder than a lion,

and restless to the bone.

My whiskers were just twitching

to set off on my own.

But I heard the words

Old Granny purred

And what she said

is how things occurred.

Granny

When life turns dark

and things look black,"

Here she buttoned my coat

and she tightened my pack.

"Just remember, dear,

That A CAT comes back."

Through all CATegories of CATaclysm there's nothing over which *some* CAT's not risen. Don't sit around and CATerwaul. CATapult back up from where you fall."

Be Ye Well

Through the whole CATalog of CATastrophe, from CATatonic to CATalepsy, the answer is CATegorically that a CAT comes back where a CAT should be."

Be Ye Well

Don't make a mountain out of a molehill.

Don't make a CATamount out of an ant.

If you want to come down

from some scary place

Don't just sit and mew, 'I can't.' "

Things are never so good

that they can't get better."

"Things are never so bad that they can't get worse."

You can't dig a hole

to get to the moon

And you can't go forward in reverse."

There's not a single road in life

Where you can see the end.

There could be kindness in an enemy,

Betrayal in a friend."

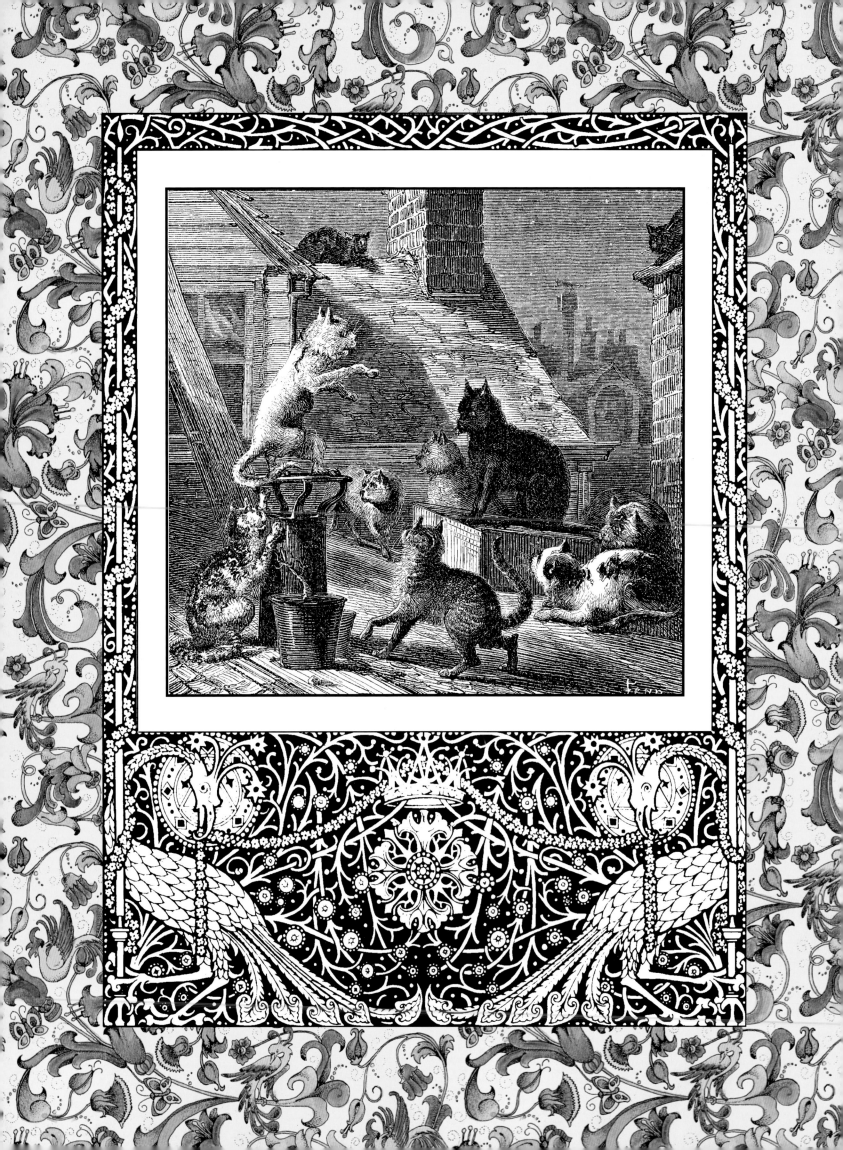

If a POLECAT betrays some confidence

Just take note don't take offense.

No CAT is PURR-fect,

Start cutting some slack.

When you're wise in your ways,

A CAT comes back."

Save today for a rainy tomorrow.

A CAT should not

Beg, steal, or borrow.

Your life must be more than

CATch as CATch can.

A wish is not a fish,

A plunge is not a plan."

When others seem

Kings and Queens of Fate

Like they're some MagnifiCAT,

And they're getting the attention,

And you're wanting some of that,

Just go on about your business, dear,

CATalyze *your* dreams to fact.

Crowned heads will often lose them

But a CAT comes back!"

Royal Catnesses

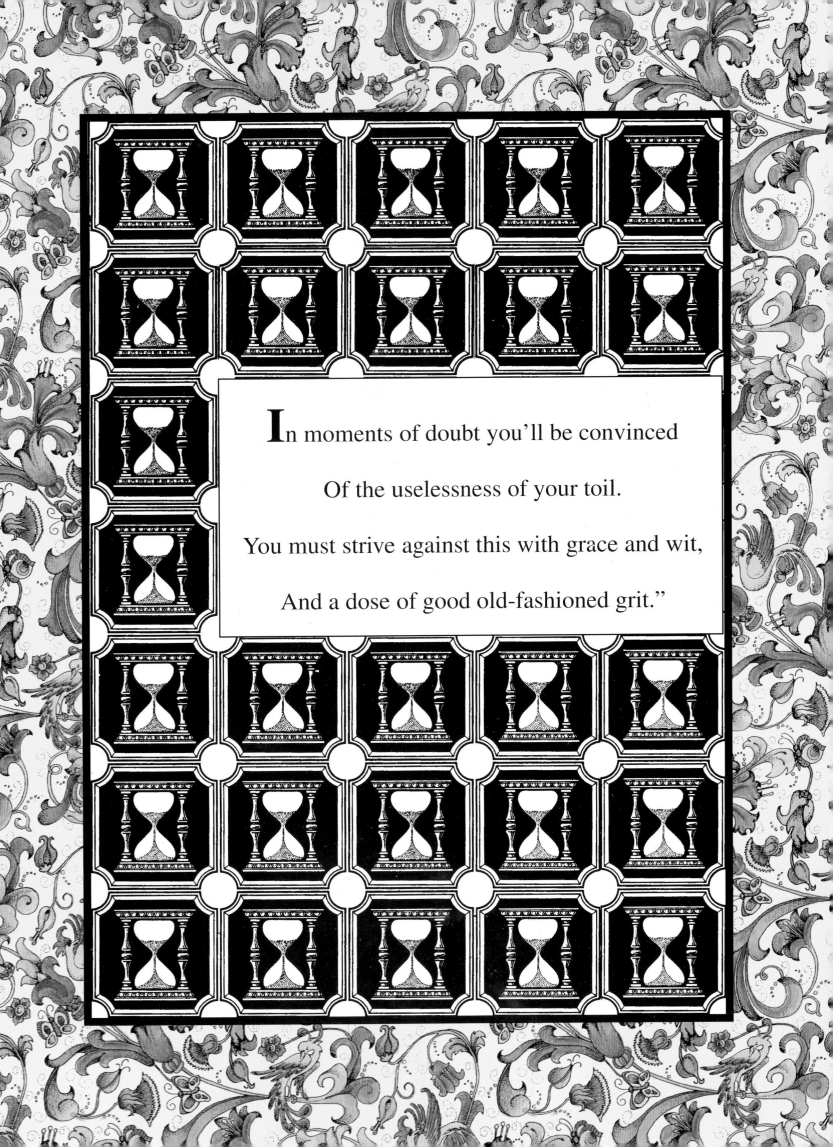

"In moments of doubt you'll be convinced

Of the uselessness of your toil.

You must strive against this with grace and wit,

And a dose of good old-fashioned grit."

And don't forget to have some fun.

With a hey-diddle-diddle

And a rummy-tum-tum!"

Whén life is coming at you fast and all seems just

within your grasp, success can be misunderstood.

Greed kills the noble and the good.

Don't be measured by what you've got.

Some things are yours, Dear, some are not."

"Your very nature,
upon occasion,
disappoints those
not of your persuasion."

Between *your* truth

and *their* truth

Will be always some middle.

Don't go *too* much your way,

And not too little!"

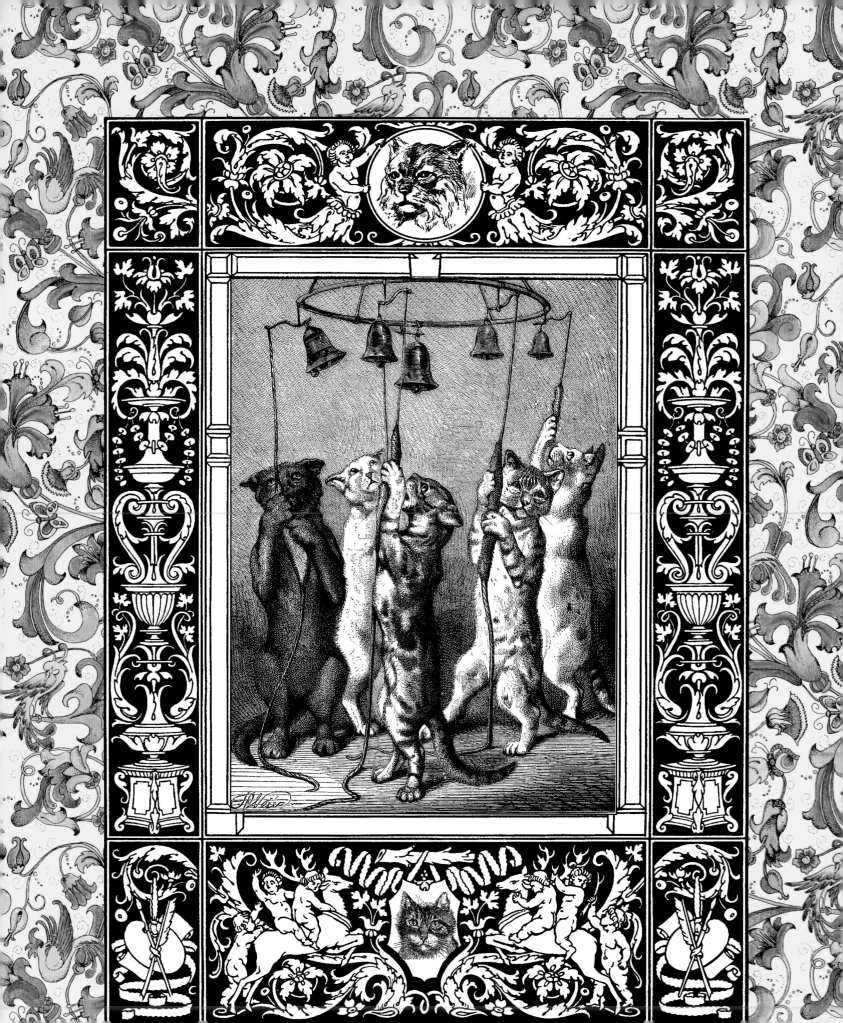

No CAT can save the world.

Work hard

But look for changes in yourself

And not in others.

This will guard you from gloom

And bell-ringers of doom."

Speak up like a CAT

When the truth must be told,

Though you shake in your boots

Let your courage be bold.

This is no time to be CAT-fraidy

Faint CAT never won fair lady."

When you've settled down

as CAT and spouse

There must be harmony

in your house.

Some pussy-footing must be done

If family peace is to be won."

When they give you a job

that can't be done,

Put your paw to the plow and do it.

You'll make mistakes

that you can't blot out.

Just know that a CAT lives through it."

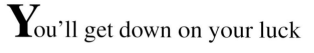

Y ou'll get down on your luck

And then deny it.

You'll know what to do

But be scared to try it.

You'll run out of steam

And off the track,

But a CAT comes back."

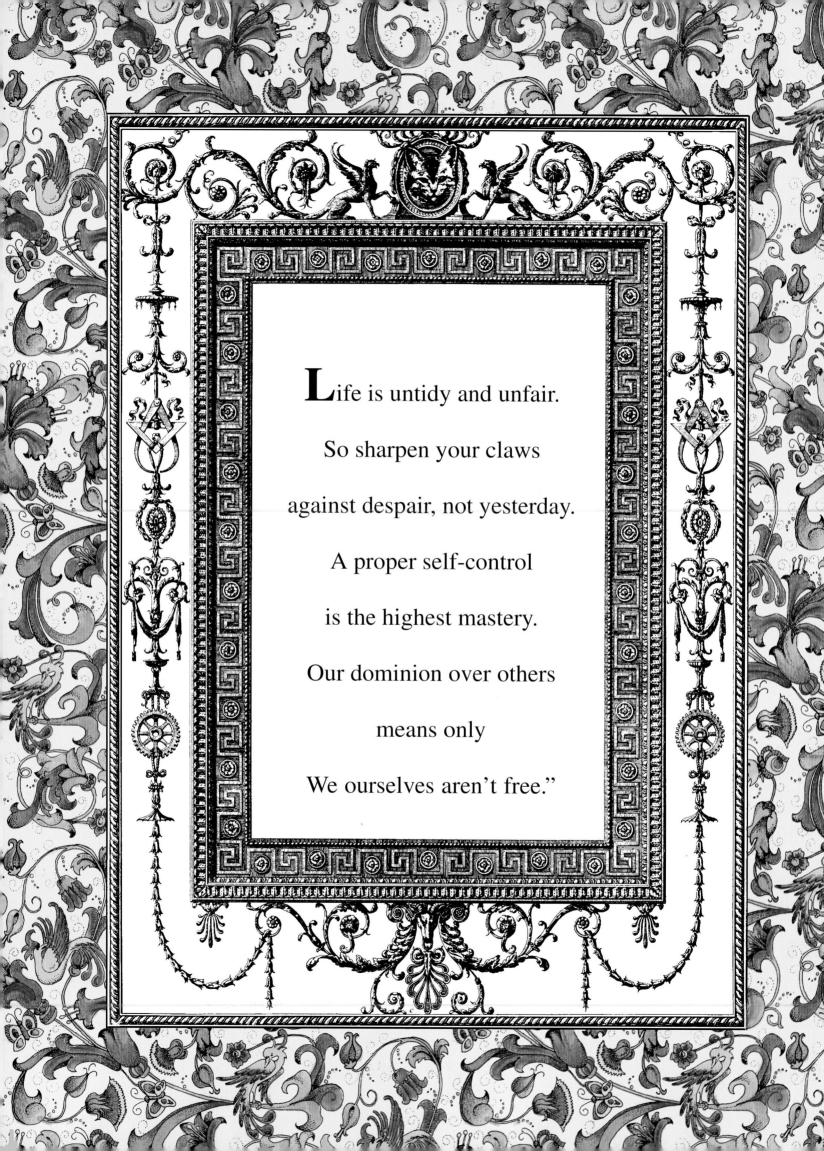

Life is untidy and unfair.

So sharpen your claws

against despair, not yesterday.

A proper self-control

is the highest mastery.

Our dominion over others

means only

We ourselves aren't free."

When you're reaching high

But you're falling low,

And life is a mystery

you don't know,

There's always something

a CAT can do.

There's always a

better point of view.

Out with the old ways

In with the new.

A CAT comes back."

These words of Granny's were straight and true

And they've served me well as they may serve you.

No matter how far you go, or wide,

And you're carrying pain and trouble inside,

If you lose it all, just begin again.

And you'll make it, nine times out of ten.

That's as right today as it was back then.

Hallelujah! A CAT comes back!

Do Good

The End